Hello Ki

Secret Santa

by Elizabeth Bennett
Illustrated by Sachiho Hino

SCHOLASTIC INC.

New York Toronto London Auckland Sydney
Mexico City New Delhi Hong Kong Buenos Aires

ISBN-13: 978-0-545-00102-1

ISBN-10: 0-545-00102-1

12 11 10 9 8 7 6 5 4 3   14 15 16 17/0

Printed in the U.S.A.   40

First printing, November 2007

It's almost Christmas vacation.

 has big news.

The class will have a Secret party.

They will each give secret to

one of their all week.

On the day of the party, they will

find out who their Secret is.

 and her each make

a to hang on their .

Their Secret can put in

their .

 makes a .

She decorates it with leaves.

 puts everyone's name in a .

All of 's reach into the .

What names do they choose?

Shhhh! It's a secret.

 reaches in.

She looks at the name she has picked.

Yippee! It's someone she really likes.

 and 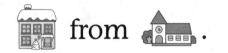 talk on the way

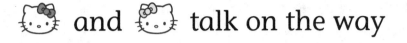 from 🏫 .

"I wonder who my Secret 🎅 is,"

🐱 says.

🐱 smiles.

"Me, too," she says.

"What should we give as 🎁 ?"

asks 🐱 .

"Let's make something," says 🐱 .

 and tell about the

Secret party.

"We are going to make ,"

 tells .

 sits at the kitchen .

 sits at her .

Both girls get busy!

 looks in her 🧦 at 🏫

the next day.

What did she get from her Secret 🎅?

A pretty 📿!

 looks in her 🧦.

She finds a beautiful 🖼.

"Who is my Secret 🎅?"

they wonder.

 and both have ideas for

their next .

 wants to bake something sweet.

 helps her with the oven.

 and Papa go to the  to buy

a treat.

 can't wait to look in her

at !

She races to her  and finds

10 .

 has  cookies in her .

"Who is my Secret ?" they wonder.

"I love being a Secret !" says .

"Me, too!" says .

They think about their last .

Both girls want to give something

very special.

The day of the Secret party

is finally here!

The class eats cookies and

drinks hot cider.

They play "Pin the Nose on the ."

Now it's time to find out who

their Secret is!

looks in her 🧦. She finds

a special 🎀.

A note says, "Merry Christmas

from 🐱."

🐱 looks in her 🧦 and finds

a fancy yellow 🎀.

"Happy Holidays from 🐱,"

says the note.

What a surprise! Playing 🎅 is fun!

Did you spot all the picture clues in this Hello Kitty book?

Each picture clue is on a flash card. Ask a grown-up to cut out the flash cards. Then try reading the words on the back of the cards. The pictures will be your clue.

Reading is fun with *Hello Kitty*!

Santa

Mr. Bearly

friends

gifts

stocking

Hello Kitty

red	desk
hat	holly
home	Mimmy

Mama	school
necklace	table
store	frame

candy canes	ten
apple	gingerbread
bow	reindeer